Beany
(Not Beanhead)
and the
Magic Crystal

To Amanda —
Enjoy!

Susan Wojciechowski

2003

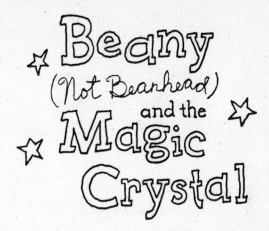

Beany
(Not Beanhead)
and the
Magic
Crystal

Susan Wojciechowski

illustrated by
Susanna Natti

CANDLEWICK PRESS
CAMBRIDGE, MASSACHUSETTS

★

*To Evan Wolfe, who taught me
the "magic" of crystals*
S. W.

*To Polly, Larry, Alex, and Carl Herz
good friends and neighbors*
S. N.

Thanks to Susanna Natti's neighbor, Carl Herz,
for his advice on Beany's drawings.

Text copyright © 1997 by Susan Wojciechowski
Illustrations copyright © 1997 by Susanna Natti

First Candlewick Press paperback edition 2001

The Library of Congress has cataloged the hardcover edition as follows:
Wojciechowski, Susan.
Beany (not Beanhead) and the magic crystal / Susan Wojciechowski ;
illustrated by Susanna Natti. — 1st ed.
Summary: Beany has a magic wishing crystal, but since it will grant only one wish,
she holds it in reserve waiting for the perfect moment to use it.
ISBN 0-7636-0052-0 (hardcover)
[1. Crystals — Fiction. 2. Schools — Fiction. 3. Friendship — Fiction.]
I. Natti, Susanna, ill. II. Title.
PZ7.W8183Bd 1997
[Fic] — dc20 96-26024

ISBN 0-7636-1441-6 (paperback)

2 4 6 8 10 9 7 5 3 1

Printed in the United States of America

This book was typeset in Bembo.

Candlewick Press
2067 Massachusetts Avenue
Cambridge, Massachusetts 02140

Contents

★ ★ ★ ★

Lost and Found

* * * *

Carol Ann is my best friend, but it's not because we're alike or anything like that. I'm quiet most of the time; Carol Ann has a big mouth. I worry about practically everything; Carol Ann hardly ever worries. I hate getting called on to do math problems at the blackboard; Carol Ann waves her hand like crazy, hoping the teacher will call on her. I guess we're best friends because we live two houses from each other and sit together on the school bus.

Here are some things I like about being best friends with Carol Ann:

1. She knows lots of interesting and weird facts, like a python snake can open its mouth wide enough to swallow a whole pig.

2. When I have a problem, she has ideas about how to solve it.

3. There are always ice cream bars in her freezer.

4. Her older sister, Margo, has makeup. When Margo isn't home we try it on.

Here are some things I don't like about her:

1. She's four months older than I am, so she bosses me around.

2. She has naturally curly hair and I don't.

3. She always has to be better than me.

Like, if I get new sneakers, she shows up the next day with sneakers that have glow-in-the-dark laces. If I say my family might go to Disney World next summer, she says she already went to Disney World and had lunch with Mickey Mouse. If I say I can swim without water wings in the deep end of the pool at the Y, she says she can do a somersault off the diving board.

This year, though, I finally got something more special than anything Carol Ann will ever have. It's so special I have never shown it to anyone but my stuffed moose, Jingle Bell, Mrs. Kasper down the street, and our class-room hamsters.

It happened because of getting lost. Most of the time getting lost is awful. I know because I've been lost three times.

The first time, I was three years old and was following my mother around at our library's used book sale, holding on to the bottom of Mom's blue coat. I let go to scratch my leg and pull up my sock because it was going down into my shoe. Then I grabbed the edge of the coat again and kept walking. When I looked up to tell my mother something, she wasn't there. At the top of the blue coat was somebody else's head. I was holding the wrong blue coat.

When my mother found me, she said I was lost for about thirty seconds, but it felt like a lot longer to me.

The second time I got lost happened in a Kmart when I was five years old. My mother was shopping for a skirt and then we were going to have ice cream at the snack bar. I got so bored I crawled into the center of the round skirt rack. I was pretending to be an Indian princess inside my tepee when all of a sudden, I heard my name called over the loudspeaker. "Bernice Sherwin-Hendricks, please come to the service desk. Your mother is waiting for you." I didn't know what a service desk was so I just sat there in my pretend tepee and cried. After a few seconds the skirts separated and a lady with a nametag that read "SAL" asked me if I was Bernice.

She handed me a tissue and stayed with me while another worker went to the service desk to get my mother. Instead of hugging me and saying how happy she was that I was found, my mother said, "Bernice Lorraine Sherwin-Hendricks, you had me worried sick. I told you not to wander off."

"But I didn't. I stayed right here by the skirts. You wandered off."

"No back talk, young lady. I am very upset with you," she said. She practically yanked me out of my tepee and held my hand all the way to the car. I never did get the ice cream.

The third time I got lost was the time it ended up being lucky. I was with my mom shopping again. This time we were in a big store that sells junk and used stuff. The store has three floors and sells just about anything you can think of. We were there because my mom wanted some old chairs to put on our porch.

Right inside the doorway was a table stacked with old magazines. My mom stopped to look through them and I started reading some old comic books on the same table. When I looked up from a Batman comic book, my mom was gone. The only person in sight was a clerk at the cash register. I never talk to strangers, but my mom said that store clerks, police officers, and anyone who talks to me when my parents are around don't count. So I called out to the lady, "My mom disappeared."

She said, "Did aliens from another planet snatch her?"

"No, I don't think so."

"Did she vanish into thin air?"

"What's thin air?"

"It's when you're looking right smack dab at somebody and they vanish."

"Then she didn't disappear into thin air but maybe into furniture."

"Well, babe, you come right over here to the counter. Rosie'll take care of everything."

She asked my name.

"It's Bernice Lorraine Sherwin-Hendricks," I said. "But most people call me Beany."

"Well, babe, I can see why. That first string of names you rattled off sure is a mouthful. Now, Beany, don't you worry about nothing. I'm going to have my husband go around the store and find out who's missing a sweet little angel with a button nose." My face got all red when she said that.

Rosie told me she wished she had a daughter just like me.

"The good Lord chose not to bless me and Pa with kids, though," she said.

I didn't know why she called her husband "Pa" when they didn't have kids. But I liked her, especially when she said, "Now, I got a job for you to do and I'll pay you one chocolate bar; that is, if your mama'll allow it. You just wash this glass case with this here spritzer bottle. Make it nice and shiny and before you're done I swear your mama will be here a-huggin' you."

I knew from Kmart that my mom wouldn't be a-huggin' me but I didn't say anything about that. I just started to clean the glass case. It was fun. I got to see everything inside and touch all of it. When I got to the bottom shelf I saw a dusty box full of things that looked like big diamonds.

"Wow!" I said. "What are these?"

"Them's crystals. They come from lights that hang over the dining room table in fancy folks' houses. When the lights are turned on, the crystals sparkle like jewels," she told me.

She held one up to the light. "Here, spritz it with the window cleaner," she said. I sprayed it and wiped it clean with a paper towel. It twinkled blue and pink and yellow.

"Most people don't know this, but some crystals have the power to grant a wish," said Rosie. She said it quietly, like it was a secret.

"Just one wish?" I asked.

"Just one."

"How do you know which crystals are wishing ones?" I asked Rosie.

"You can't tell by looking at them. You don't know till you make a wish."

I wanted a crystal so badly, but I didn't ask. I knew they would cost too much. So I gently put the crystal back in the box and finished cleaning the glass case.

This time when my mother came to get me she just sighed. She didn't even yell. She acted like she was getting used to me disappearing.

We started to walk away when Rosie called out, "You forgot your pay, babe. You can have either the candy or a crystal. Take your pick."

I couldn't believe my ears. I looked at my mother. She nodded.

Quickly, before she or Rosie could change her mind, I took the crystal that I had cleaned. I had a feeling it was a wishing one.

I stayed right next to Mom the whole

time she was picking out her chairs and paying for them. I didn't get bored. I didn't complain that I was tired. I didn't ask her fifty times if she was through yet. I just stood there smiling, feeling the crystal in my pocket.

When we got home I put a piece of blue yarn through the hole in the top of the crystal and put it around my neck. I decided I would wear it always so that when just the right time came to make a wish, I would have it ready. I tucked the crystal inside my shirt so no one would see it. I couldn't show anyone. They might talk me into wishing for something for them. Or Kevin Gates might just yank it right off my neck and make a wish before I could even tell Ms. Babbitt.

Then Jingle Bell and I went to Mrs. Kasper's house. Mrs. Kasper is an old lady who lives alone down the street from me. Some kids in the neighborhood are scared of her because it is very dark in her house and because her skin doesn't fit her. It is very wrinkly and loose. I like her, though. Whenever I visit her, we sit at her dining room table that's covered with a lace tablecloth, and she serves me a tiny cup of tea and a chocolate-covered cherry. The first time she gave me one, I bit it, then put it down on the lace tablecloth. When I picked it up again, I saw that it had leaked sticky red cherry syrup on the lace. I was scared to tell her, so I covered the spot with my teacup. Mrs. Kasper never said anything about it, but now she puts my candy on a plate.

Mrs. Kasper is very fancy, so I thought she might know about crystals and how to tell a wishing one. She is so fancy she always wears a dress and stockings and calls me "child" instead of Beany. After tea and a chocolate-covered cherry on a plate, I showed

Mrs. Kasper the crystal and told her all about it. She looked it over very carefully, but said she couldn't tell if it was a wishing one or not.

That night I put the crystal under my pillow. As I lay in bed I thought about all the things I could wish for. I could wish for curly hair or that my freckles would disappear. I could wish for all As on my report card. I could wish that I wouldn't be afraid of Kevin Gates, who always pushes ahead of me in line, even when I'm line leader. I could wish for anything in the whole world. I had to be very careful about the wish, though. I had only one chance and I couldn't waste it on something stupid, like glow-in-the-dark sneaker laces.

That's when I realized that I finally had something more special than Carol Ann. Carol Ann might have had lunch with Mickey Mouse, but I had a wishing crystal. I didn't even care that she would never know about it. I knew about it and that was all that mattered.

The Trophy

* * * *

The first time I thought about making a wish on my crystal was when my class had a contest. The prize was a trophy and I have wanted a trophy for a long time.

My brother, Philip, who's thirteen, has eight trophies. I have none. Philip has so many trophies that my father built a shelf in his room just to hold them all. When my father built it, I asked him to put up a trophy shelf in my room, too. But my shelf just sat there empty till my mother finally filled it with a bunch of my stuffed animals. Then it looked full, but in my mind it was still empty, if you know what I mean.

I did get a bowling trophy once, but that one doesn't count. Carol Ann and I were in Junior Bowl-A-Roll for a year and I won a tiny trophy of a woman rolling a bowling ball. It was called a Participation Award, which means I was a loser at bowling but I showed up every week.

In case you're wondering why the trophy isn't on my shelf, Carol Ann and I were tossing it back and forth on our way home from the awards lunch and it fell. The woman's arm with the bowling ball broke off. So I sold it (the trophy, not the arm) at a yard sale for ten cents. Mikey next door bought it. He's four and has more trophies than me.

Then came the contest in our classroom. It was my big chance to finally win a real trophy. My teacher, Ms. Babbitt, tries to teach us other stuff besides math and spelling and junk like that. She tries to teach us about caring for the earth and being polite and being nice to one another. She doesn't have any kids of her own, so she thinks even boys can be polite. She doesn't know my brother. He could win the trophy for World's Rudest Human Being. Right now he is practicing how to talk while burping. Anyway, Ms. Babbitt came up with the idea that we would have a Caring and Sharing Contest.

One day she came to school wearing her smiley-face earrings, the ones she wears whenever she has a surprise or something special planned. As soon as we saw the earrings we started asking her what the surprise was, so she told us about the contest.

"We're going to see who can be the caringest and sharingest student during the whole month," she said. "The winner will

receive a trophy called a loving cup. I will
have the winner's name put at the bottom."
She held up an awesome trophy. It was a tall
gold cup with handles on the sides.

"How do we win?" asked Allison.

"Each time you do a caring or sharing
act, write it on a piece of paper and put it in
a box that I'll keep on my desk. At the end
of the month I'll name the winner."

Then she had us write down all the ways we could think of to be caring and sharing. I put:

1. Tell Ms. Babbitt she looks pretty.

2. Trade my Twinkie for Carol Ann's apple at lunch.

3. Let kids get ahead of me in line.

4. Let my cousin Laura wear my ballerina costume when we play, even though she looks stupid in it.

Before I could write any more Ms. Babbitt collected our lists and read some of them to the class so we could get lots of ideas.

Some of the suggestions were dumb, like "Love everyone." It is impossible to love everyone, especially Kevin Gates when he walks up to me in the bus line after school and totally unzips my backpack so that all the books and stuff fall out and then yells, "You dropped something, clumsy."

From my list Ms. Babbitt read the part about telling her she looks pretty. "I like that one," said Ms. Babbitt. She fluffed up her hair as she said it. Everyone laughed. My face got all red. I wondered if they were laughing at Ms. Babbitt or at my idea.

Ms. Babbitt put the trophy on top of her file cabinet, where we could all look at it and drool over it for the next month.

On the bus ride home I told Carol Ann she shouldn't even try to win because it wouldn't do her any good. I was going to be the most caringest and sharingest person on the planet earth. Maybe that was the wrong thing to say, because Carol Ann answered, "Wanna bet?" Then she stood up and shoved me over to the window seat. She sat in the aisle seat and pulled out a sheet of filler

paper from her backpack. She folded it into
eight sections and ripped them apart. On
one piece she wrote:

Gave window seat on bus to someone.
—Carol Ann

She put the pieces in her backpack and sat
there grinning. It got me so mad I couldn't
help myself. I kicked her leg. She said, "I

forgive you," then pulled out another of the pieces of paper and wrote:

Forgave someone for kicking me.
                                   —Carol Ann

Carol Ann is my best friend, but sometimes I don't really like her that much.

At dinner that night I told my family about the contest and asked them if they would tell me ways I could be more caring and sharing. My mom said I didn't need a contest. I was always caring and sharing anyway. My dad told me I could start by giving him my slice of chocolate cake. When I pushed my plate over to him, he laughed and said he was just kidding. Philip told me the only thing he wanted me to share with him was my bank account.

For the rest of the month I cleared the

table before Mom had to ask. I didn't tell on Philip when I heard him bet his friend Max that he could go a week without changing his socks. I ate my father's chili without making a face.

In school, the kids in my class tried to beat one another for the trophy. We emptied Ms. Babbitt's wastebasket every few minutes. We clapped erasers. We erased the blackboard every time Ms. Babbitt wrote on it. We told her she looked pretty. Every day Ms. Babbitt got flowers. Every day she got apples, too.

One of the ideas Ms. Babbitt had read to the class was "Visit people who are sick or alone." So I tried to visit Mrs. Kasper every day. While I had tea and a chocolate-covered cherry we talked. Mostly, she talked about her dead husband, Walter; only, instead of dead, she said "dear departed."

Every time I did something nice I wrote

it on a bit of paper and put it in the caring and sharing box. I noticed that Carol Ann put a lot of notes in the box, too.

One day I got a great idea. My mom was planting flowers in our backyard garden. I asked her if she would have any extras that I could plant under the windows outside my classroom. Mom gave me six pansy plants. I figured I'd plant them after school on the last day of the month and put one caring and sharing paper in the box for each pansy I planted.

I was smiling and singing out loud as I dragged the plants outside after school on the last day of the contest.

"What are you doing?" I heard over my shoulder. It was Carol Ann, butting into my plan.

"Nothing," I answered.

"Here, let me help," she said.

Every time I dug a hole, she grabbed a pansy and set it in. As I was packing dirt around the last one, Carol Ann's mom came to take her to a dentist appointment. Carol Ann quickly pulled a square of paper from her pocket and wrote on it.

"Here, put this in the caring and sharing box, will you?" she asked as she ran to her car. I put the paper in my backpack so I wouldn't lose it while I put my shovel, the pots, and my watering can in a box and took them inside school. I wrote out six caring and sharing notes for the six pansies I had planted and put the notes in the box. I had to run to catch the late bus.

The next day we all sat nervously as Ms. Babbitt took the trophy from the file cabinet and put it on her desk. Her smiley-face earrings swung from side to side as she looked from one end of the room to the other, smil-

ing at each of us. I was so nervous I closed my
eyes. I wiggled in my seat and bit my nails
as I waited to hear who would get the trophy.

"I am so proud," Ms. Babbitt said. "You all
deserve this award. You have all shown what
special children you are. Of course, you know
that all of you are winners, but only one person can take this award home today. Because
the final count was so close, before I name
the winner I would like to give an award to

the person who did the second highest number of caring and sharing acts—Carol Ann." Ms. Babbitt gave Carol Ann a certificate. "And now, our winner, the caringest and sharingest student—Bernice."

I screamed. I jumped out of my seat and almost tripped over Kevin Gates's foot sticking out in the aisle as I ran to the front of the room to get to my trophy. The class clapped. Boomer Fenton whistled.

When I got home I pushed all the stuffed animals off my trophy shelf and put the loving cup right in the middle. After supper I brought everyone upstairs to admire the award. Mom hugged me. Dad gave me the thumbs up sign. Philip said, "I'll buy it off you for a buck."

"No way," I told him. "The trophy is never moving off that spot." We all went out for ice cream to celebrate.

When we got back home I sat down at the dining room table to do my spelling homework. I unzipped the little pocket of my backpack to get a pencil. A piece of paper fell out. I read it. It said:

Planted flowers at school.
—Carol Ann

I stared at the note for a long time. Then I started to cry. I cried because I knew that if I had told Carol Ann to make one note for each pansy like I had, and if I'd turned in her notes, she would have won. Ms. Babbitt had said the count was very close. I went to my room and looked at the shelf. Even though there was a trophy on it, the shelf was really empty, if you know what I mean.

In bed that night I held Jingle Bell in one hand and my wishing crystal in the other. I decided to wish that if I told Ms. Babbitt the truth she would say, "Telling the truth was truly the caringest thing anyone could do. I have decided that you should keep the trophy. We will not say anything about this to the rest of the class." I got out of bed and put the crystal around my neck. I held it tight and started to say, "I wish . . ." but then I stopped. I realized that if I used my wish it would be gone. What if this wasn't the absolute perfect moment? What if I used up my wish and a more perfect moment came up later? I couldn't bring myself to use up the wish yet. I decided to save it.

The next day I came downstairs early, while my mom was having what she calls her sunrise cup of tea. I squeezed myself onto her lap, between her and the newspaper she was reading. I pretended to read the comics with her, but when a tear fell onto the page, Mom closed the paper and turned my head to hers.

"What's wrong, Beany?" she asked.

I told her about Carol Ann and the pansies. I asked her what I should do.

"I think you know what you have to do, Bean."

"Yeah," I answered, twirling the tie of her ratty blue robe around my fingers.

"You know something?" my mom said as

she kissed the top of my head. "You are one pretty special kid."

She drove me to school early. I bit my nails the whole way. When I told Ms. Babbitt about the pansies, I couldn't look at her. I stared at a black spot on the floor the whole time. I put the trophy on her desk and turned to go to my seat.

"Come here, Beany," said Ms. Babbitt. She put her arm around me. "Telling the truth was truly the caringest thing anyone could do. I am prouder of you right now than I have ever been of a student in all my years of teaching. I do have to give the trophy to Carol Ann and present you with a certificate; I hope you understand that. But in my heart there are two winners." Ms. Babbitt hugged me. She smelled like soap. I felt good inside.

When the bell rang for school to start,

Ms. Babbitt announced that there had been an error in the counting and that Carol Ann had won and I had come in second. The class clapped for Carol Ann. Boomer Fenton whistled. I smiled and clapped, too.

Through my shirt I touched the crystal. I didn't have the trophy but I still had a wish to make when the perfect moment came.

Hamsters

★ ★ ★ ★

We have hamsters in our classroom and I almost had to use up my wish because of them.

Our hamsters used to be named Bert and Ernie. But then they had babies, so we had a contest to pick new names. Now they are called Kermit and Miss Piggy. Every weekend someone gets to take them home. I was nervous that when it got to be my turn, my parents wouldn't let me take them because Philip is allergic. That means animal fur and feathers make him sneeze.

His problem started two years ago when

my cousin Laura asked me to take care of her parakeet, Pippin, while her family went away on vacation. We brought Pippin home and after a few minutes, Philip started to sneeze. He sneezed fourteen times in one minute.

My mother got all worried and made me take the bird to Carol Ann's house. For two weeks she got to watch Pippin ring his bell and kiss himself in the mirror and say, "Pippin wants a Cool Ranch Dorito," which is the only thing Pippin has ever said.

When my relatives got back from vacation they paid Carol Ann. While Carol Ann put the money in a gray metal box she keeps under her bed she told me about all the fun she had with Pippin, like the time he went to the bathroom on Carol Ann's sister Margo's shoulder and Margo got hysterical. For that alone Carol Ann should have paid my cousin.

A couple of weeks before it was my turn to take Kermit and Miss Piggy home for the weekend, I asked Carol Ann if she had any ideas on how I could get my parents to let me do it. Carol Ann is always full of ideas.

Carol Ann told me she had a plan. She said, "First, you ask your parents if you can have a horse for a pet. There's no way they'll say yes to that. Then you ask them if you can have a snake. Of course they'll say no again. After that you say, 'Well then, can I have a tarantula spider for a pet?' Your mother will practically faint because she hates crawly things of all kinds. Finally you say, 'Well, can I at least keep our classroom hamsters for a weekend?' After the horse, the snake, and the spider ideas, the hamsters will seem like nothing and they'll say yes. They won't even care about Philip's sneezing. Trust me. It'll work like a charm."

The plan did not work like a charm. When I got to the hamster part my father said, "I smell a rat."

"They're not rats and they don't smell," I said.

Dad laughed and told me that "I smell a rat" means "I suspect I'm being tricked."

"Did Carol Ann have anything to do with this?" Mom asked.

"Well, sort of. She was helping me because she knows I want those hamsters more than anything in the whole, whole, whole world. Please let me babysit them. I'll do anything if you let me. I'll make my bed every day for the next hundred years. I'll eat everything you put on my plate even if it tastes gross. Please, please, with gummy bears on top?"

"Well," said my mother, thinking it over, "I'm not sure you're responsible enough to take good care of the hamsters. Remember

the time you watched your friend Judy's
goldfish and while you were changing its
water you let it slide down the sink drain?"

"That was when I was just a little kid," I
said. "It doesn't count."

Then my mother surprised me. She said I
could take my weekend if I kept Kermit and
Miss Piggy in my room with the door shut and
always washed my hands after touching them.

"But if Philip starts to sneeze, you'll have

to take them to Carol Ann's. Do you understand?" she added.

I didn't understand. I mean, what's the big deal about sneezing? Sneezing never killed anybody. Sneezing is fun. Just ask Kevin Gates in my class. Every time he has to sneeze he tries to do it as loud as he can. Everybody laughs. Except Ms. Babbitt. But I didn't say all that stuff to my mother. I just agreed with her.

The night before I brought home the hamsters I made a big sign for my door that said:

Welcome to My Room (Except Philip)

Then I knocked on my brother's bedroom door.

"Yeah?" he said.

"Can I come in?"

"I'm busy. What do you want, Beanhead?"

He always calls me that. I hate it.

"I want to give you some money," I answered.

Philip opened the door a few inches and stuck out his hand.

"Let me in first," I said. "You have to promise me something for the money."

I asked Philip to promise that he wouldn't sneeze when Kermit and Miss Piggy were at our house. I offered to pay him a dollar.

Philip put down the comic book he was reading.

"Beanhead, I don't sneeze around animals because I want to. I sneeze because my nose gets itchy and stuffed up. If you gave me a million dollars I couldn't stop."

"Oh," I said. "Well, then could you spend this weekend in your tent in the yard?"

"Yeah, right. For you, two rats, and a dollar I'll gladly freeze to death. Scram. I'm busy," he said and went back to reading his comic book, which he does practically all the time, except when he's lifting weights or looking at himself in the mirror or talking on the phone with his friend Will.

The next day Mom and I brought Kermit and Miss Piggy's cage home in the back of our van. Mom carried the cage, which is really a fish aquarium with wood shavings in it, to my room while I followed with the

supplies. I talked to the hamsters so they wouldn't feel scared.

Mom put the cage on my floor. We put a piece of screen on top of it and put a book on top of the screen, just like Ms. Babbitt taught us to do, because hamsters like to escape. Mom told me to leave them alone for a while so they could calm down and get used to their new surroundings. She warned me that whenever I did open the cage I should always remember to put the screen back and hold it down with a book.

After supper I went to my room.

"Hi, Kermit. Hi, Miss Piggy," I said. "Welcome to my room." I showed them my desk and my bookshelves. I showed them my crystal. I told them I hoped they wouldn't mind the pile of dirty clothes on the floor. Then I introduced the hamsters to Jingle Bell. I told them they could tell Jingle Bell anything, even their secrets, because Jingle Bell is a good listener and never tells secrets to other people, like Carol Ann sometimes does. Once I told her I thought my ears were too big and the very next day Kevin Gates called me Dumbo during recess. I knew Carol Ann had told him on the bus.

I opened the hamsters' cage and petted them. Their fur was gold and soft. I put food pellets and some ripped-up lettuce in their cage and filled their water tube. I put the screen on top of the cage and went to listen at Philip's door for sneezing.

When it was bedtime I tiptoed into my room. I got ready for bed in the dark so I wouldn't bother Kermit and Miss Piggy.

The next morning I was up at six A.M. I didn't want to miss even a second of my weekend with the hamsters. I had big plans for the day.

When I looked into the cage I couldn't see the hamsters.

"Come out, come out, wherever you are," I said and poked on the glass near the pile of wood shavings in the corner of the aquarium. Nothing moved. That was when I noticed that the screen was not completely covering the aquarium. It had been moved. There was no book on top of the screen, either. The

book was on my desk. I figured the hamsters couldn't have put it there, so it must have been me. I must have forgotten to put it back on the cage after I fed them the night before.

I poked around in the wood shavings just to make sure Kermit and Miss Piggy weren't playing a trick on me. I searched under my bed and in my pile of dirty clothes. I looked in my closet and in my dresser drawers. I looked in my wastebasket.

Usually I scream at the top of my lungs when anything goes wrong. But this time I just sat on the floor for a while, shaking. I was so scared of what Ms. Babbitt would say when she found out I lost the hamsters. No one else had ever lost them before. I would probably get a big black **X** on my report card in the part called "Follows Directions."

Finally I had to tell my family. All of us except Philip, who stayed in his room to keep from sneezing, looked for the hamsters. All day Saturday we looked for the hamsters. All day Sunday we looked for the hamsters. Carol Ann came over to help, but all she did was get me more worried. She kept saying things like, "How can you show your face in school Monday if we don't find them?" and, "Boy, is Ms. Babbitt going to be mad." I finally told her to go home.

By Sunday night I knew I would have to

use my wish to get the hamsters back. I
would have to use up a perfectly good wish
just to get out of trouble. If the crystal
turned out not to be the wishing kind I
would have to ask my parents if we could
move, because I could not keep going to my
school. I could not face Ms. Babbitt and
my class every day and have them look at me

funny and have Kevin Gates call me mean names.

Just as I was telling all this to Jingle Bell, my father yelled up the stairs, "I think I found them!"

My mother and I rushed into the family room, where we heard scratching sounds coming from behind one of the walls.

"They got into the heating ducts," Dad said. Heating ducts are metal tubes inside the walls that bring heat from the furnace into the rooms.

Dad used a screwdriver to get the cover off the heating duct. He pushed a long piece of rope into the opening. Dad said the hamsters probably got stuck in a spot where they couldn't climb up. The rope would give them something to grab on to. Dad turned the cage on its side in front of the hole in the wall.

After a few minutes Miss Piggy crawled out of the duct and into her cage. Kermit was right behind her. I jumped up and down and cheered.

We took the cage upstairs. I put volume A

and volume M of our encyclopedia on top of the screen, just to be safe.

"I'm sorry your weekend with the hamsters turned out this way, Beany," said Mom.

"Yeah, but just think, pretty soon it'll be my turn again. Can I bring them home when my turn comes again? Please? Please?"

Dad hit me over the head with my pillow. My parents left. When we were alone I told the hamsters how worried I had been. I told them how I almost had to use up my wish to find them. But I forgave them for escaping. They were just being hamsters. And I bet they had more fun at our house than at anybody else's.

I sat by their cage for a few minutes and watched them play. Then I went to bed. I couldn't wait for my next turn to have Kermit and Miss Piggy for a weekend.

School Pictures

* * * *

School pictures stink. On picture day I have to wear a frilly party dress that's itchy and scratchy, and no one is allowed to go to the playground during lunchtime because we might get dirty or sweaty. When it's our class's turn for pictures, we go to the gym and stand in a long line while parent volunteers keep yelling, "All right, that's enough noise! Keep it down!" No one listens to them because they're just parents, not teachers. The only good thing about school pictures is that you get a free comb.

So on the day that Ms. Babbitt handed

out booklets telling about school pictures, I groaned. A bunch of other kids did, too. Ms. Babbitt pretended to be surprised.

"Why, children," she said, "I should think you would want a special memory of our year together. I, for one, would like a wallet-size photo of each and every one of you. Promise you'll save one for me?"

We all said, "Yes, Ms. Babbitt." (Except for Kevin Gates, who yelled out, "You must have an awful big wallet!") But really, Ms. Babbitt would not want a picture of me in her wallet. My school pictures are disasters. My first year in school I tried to smile a really big smile for my picture. When my brother saw it, he said I looked like someone was ordering me to smile at gunpoint. My mouth was smiling but the rest of my face looked scared. So the next year I didn't smile and my pictures looked like wanted posters.

The following year the photographer's helper, who checks each kid right before the picture is taken to make sure the kid doesn't have anything hanging out of his nose or some hair sticking straight up, combed my hair for me. She parted my hair in the wrong place and combed it straight over to one side. That year Carol Ann told me my picture looked like I was from the planet Forehead.

On the bus ride from school Carol Ann was all excited picking out which background she wanted. There are a bunch of neat backgrounds to choose from, with names like "winter wonderland," "forest glade," and "up, up and away," which means clouds. Carol Ann decided on "autumn in the country" because the colors went with her hair. Carol Ann has curly blonde hair that she thinks is the most beautiful hair in the world. She's always shaking her head around to make the curls bounce.

"I hate school pictures," I said to Carol Ann.

"I like school pictures," Carol Ann said, flipping her curls. "I'm ordering the deluxe package. Look at this. One 11×14. Three

8x10s. Five 5x7s. Twenty-four wallet size. Which package are you getting?"

"The smallest one, I guess," I mumbled.

"It's because of your freckles, isn't it?" Carol Ann said.

"What's wrong with my freckles?" I asked her.

"Oh, nothing. It's just that my grandmother has freckles on her hands and she's always putting cream on them to get rid of them, but they just keep getting bigger. She doesn't call them freckles, though. When they're on your hands they're called liver spots. My grandmother says if you don't use the cream the spots keep getting bigger till they all join together."

I slumped down in my seat and bit my nails for the rest of the bus ride. When I got home, I ran up to the bathroom, locked the door, and looked at myself in the big mirror

over the sink. I saw the same old me with
short brown hair that always sticks up in
weird ways, depending how I sleep on it. I
saw the same old ears that stick out like radar
dishes. I inherited them from my dad, who
says it's a blessing because we can hear everything that's being said within a ten-mile
range. He thinks it's funny, but it's not. And

I saw my freckles. I counted them. Twenty-three, same as always. I stared at myself for a long time trying to see if they were bigger than yesterday. I decided that one of them, a freckle on my nose, looked like it was growing.

I needed some liver spot cream, fast. I ran to Mrs. Kasper's house. After we sat down at the dining room table and she brought out the box of cherries, I asked her if she had any.

"No, child, I don't," Mrs. Kasper said.

"But aren't you worried that your liver spots will spread into giant liver blobs?"

"At my age I have more important things to worry about. Why are you interested in liver spot cream?"

"I need some," I said. "I want to get rid of my freckles."

"Child," she said as she poured tea, "your freckles are a part of what makes you special."

"They are not special, they're ugly. Carol Ann thinks so and so does Philip. He says my face looks like a connect-the-dots game."

Mrs. Kasper asked me why I was suddenly so concerned. I told her about the school pictures.

"I hate school pictures," I said.

"Let me show you something," said Mrs. Kasper. She went into the living room and came back with a gold-framed picture of herself and her dear departed husband. In it they were standing in the yard, squinting at the sun. Mr. Kasper was sort of fat and mostly bald, but he had a big smile on his face. So did Mrs. Kasper. It surprised me to see her smile because she usually seems sad.

"If my dear departed Walter had hated pictures, I wouldn't have this," said Mrs. Kasper. "It was taken one week before he departed from this earth. Not a day goes by that I don't look at this photo. It helps me remember every line in his face and every liver spot on his hands. They are as dear to me as gold. Now you go on home and stop worrying about school pictures. They will turn out just fine."

On the day before school pictures, I finally told Carol Ann my reasons for not wanting my picture taken. I made her promise not to tell anyone. I made her cross her heart, her arms, her legs, and her eyes to prove she meant it. Then I told her it was my freckles, my big ears, and my hair that I was worried about.

"Is that all?" Carol Ann said and laughed. "I can help you with all that. Just leave it to me."

That night Carol Ann came to my house with a plastic bag full of tiny rollers that fastened with rubber bands. She said they were the ones her grandmother used when she gave herself a home permanent. Her grandmother's hair is very frizzy, but I didn't say anything about that. I let Carol Ann put about a hundred rollers in my hair. We did it in my room so Philip wouldn't tease me and my mother wouldn't say something like, "Beany your hair is beautiful just the way it is." Sometimes mothers don't understand.

The next morning I got up an hour early

and went to Carol Ann's house. She tried to take the rollers out of my hair. She could barely get them out, my hair was so tangled up in the rubber bands. She tried to comb my hair, but she couldn't get a comb to go through it. Two combs broke. Finally she combed it with her fingers, but even they couldn't get through the hair, it was so curly. I kept yelling "Ouch, ooch, ouch" the whole time.

Next, she inspected my freckles.

"We can cover these with marker. My mother has a white one she uses at the library to write on books. It's the kind that won't wash off, so you won't have to worry if it rains today." Carol Ann colored each of my freckles with the white marker.

The last thing Carol Ann did was to tape my ears back with wide gray tape like the kind my father has in his toolbox. She wrapped the tape around the back of my head and tried to cover it with my hair. "Just keep your head aimed straight at the camera at all times. If you don't turn sideways, the tape won't show," she told me.

When she was finished she looked at me for a long time before she said, "Don't look in the mirror. Let's let the pictures be a surprise." Carol Ann was not smiling. She looked sort of worried. She grabbed my arm and pulled me toward the door. I pulled away and when I looked in the bathroom mirror, I let out a scream I know could be heard in the next time zone.

I did not look like I was from the planet Forehead, I looked like I was from the planet Freak. My hair looked like a giant ball of brown cotton candy. It looked just like Binky's, the clown who did balloon tricks at my fifth birthday party. On my face were twenty-three bright white dots. They looked like some kind of disease. The tape that held my ears down flat made a huge dent in the frizz on the back of my head.

Carol Ann's mother, father, sister, and grandparents, who live with them, all came running to the bathroom to find out what the screaming was about. When Carol Ann's mother saw me, she ran out of the room. Her grandmother sat down on the toilet lid and started to fan herself with a towel. Everyone else just stared.

If there was ever a perfect time to use my wish, this was it. I asked everyone to leave. As I stood at the mirror holding my crystal and trying to figure out the exact words to use to undo the mess Carol Ann had made of me, I heard my mother's voice outside the bathroom door. Carol Ann's mother must have called her on the phone.

"Beany, honey," she said, "let's go home."

My mother tried to fix my head. To get the tape off, she did some pulling and some cutting and lots of mumbling and grumbling under her breath about Carol Ann. The pulling part hurt.

Then she put some bad-smelling stuff on a cotton ball and dabbed at the white marker covering my freckles and did some more mumbling and grumbling. I stayed home from school so I could go to the hairdresser and get my hair styled. Usually we can't get an appointment on the same day, but I heard Mom use the word "emergency" on the phone and we got an appointment for noon.

Two weeks later I had my picture taken on makeup day, the day when kids who'd been absent could have them taken. The photographer had his shirt buttoned crooked and I noticed it just when he was taking one

of my pictures. I laughed as he snapped the camera.

When my pictures came, Mom said, "Now, there's a Beany smile." I guess a Beany smile is good, because she ordered the deluxe package.

I gave a wallet-size picture to Carol Ann, but she didn't have any to trade. Her parents didn't order any pictures. They said she looked worried in all of them. I guess she was thinking about what she had done to me while her pictures were being taken.

"I hate school pictures," Carol Ann said when I gave her one of mine.

"I like school pictures," I said as I looked at the one I was giving her. The Beany smile looked nice. And I didn't even have to use my wish to get it. I could save my wish for the perfect moment.

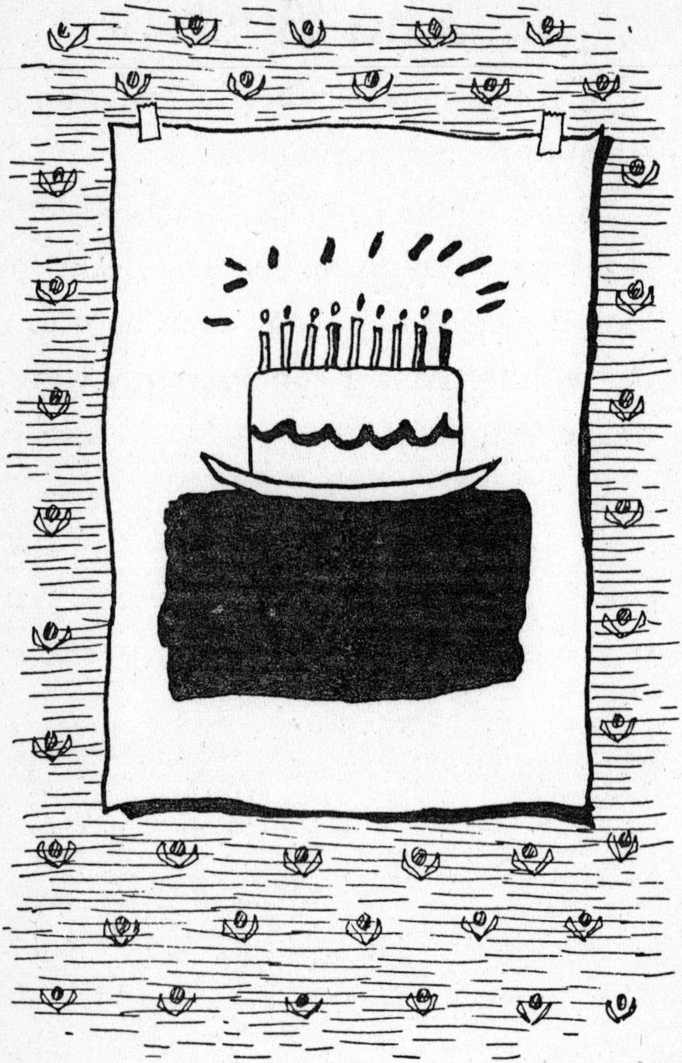

The Wish

* ★ * ★ *

My birthday is June 15. That is the best time for a birthday because the weather is warm enough to have my party outside, and my friends and I can run around and yell without giving my mother a headache, but summer vacation hasn't started yet, so it can be celebrated at school, too.

Whenever someone has a birthday in Ms. Babbitt's class she makes it special. She wears her earrings that look like wrapped presents. She lets the birthday person hold the flag for the pledge, be the messenger, be line leader, and choose a game to play before dismissal.

She also lets the birthday person take treats to other teachers. I take treats to the office, the nurse, the library lady, the gym teacher, the music teacher, and the art teacher. I walk real slow.

I started planning my party way ahead of time. My mother told me I could invite eight friends, so I decided to mail the invitations, not hand them out at school like some kids do. I didn't want the ones who weren't invited to feel bad.

I also decided I would not do what Carol Ann did before her party in February. For one month before her party she got her own way all the time. On the playground she told me she would not invite me to her party if I didn't let her have the swing when it was my turn, and I had been waiting ten minutes in the cold to get it. In the cafeteria she told me she would not invite me if I didn't give her my dessert. In class she told me she would not invite me if I didn't let her be my partner for a science project. I was very happy when Carol Ann's party was finally over.

Two weeks before my party I mailed the invitations. Then I waited for people to let me know if they could come. That is a very hard part about having a party. I always worry that no one will want to come. Everyone except Jess said they could be there.

After that I made a list of the gifts I wanted, just in case anyone asked. I wrote:

Barbie stuff, jewelry, makeup, candy, and a horse.

I did not show the list to my mom. If I did, she would have said, "No makeup,"

even though I only wanted it for play.

A week before the party my mom and I planned the food. We decided on spaghetti, ice cream cake, juice, red licorice, chocolate kisses, and popcorn. We bought plates, cups, and napkins with stars all over them. We bought favors. I chose wax lips, pencils that said Happy Birthday on them, and stickers.

When the day of the party came I was very nervous. I worried that no one would show up. I worried that, if they did, they would all have a rotten time and talk about it in school on Monday. I worried that they wouldn't like the food or that they would think my games were stupid. I worried they would hate the favors. I worried I might burst out crying if all my presents were dumb. I got nervous that my mother would make me wear my school picture dress instead of the shorts and shirt I had picked out. Finally I decided that having a party was not such a good idea after all, and I asked my mother to call everyone and tell them I was sick.

"Beany," my mother said, "remember your party last year? You got so worked up you gave yourself a stomachache. And what happened in the end? The party was fun. This one will be, too." Mom hugged me and went back to making meatballs.

I went to my room and changed from my pajamas to my party shorts. I put my crystal around my neck and tucked it inside my shirt, just like I've done every single day since I got it from Rosie. I lay on my bed and tried to read *Stuart Little* but I couldn't keep my mind on it. I kept worrying about my party. I even thought about not leaving my room when the party started. I could tie myself to my bedpost so my parents couldn't drag me out.

I got so nervous and scared I finally decided that this was the right time to use my wish. I would wish for a perfect birthday. I sat down at my desk and started to write out my birthday wish, since it was going to be a very long one. I wrote:

I wish that my birthday party will be perfect and that everyone will come and give me great stuff and have a great time and not think any of the games are stupid and I'll get a horse as a gift from my parents.

I wondered if that was too much to put into one wish. Maybe none of it would happen if I got too greedy. I erased the part about the games.

"Beany," my mother called up the stairs. "Would you come down here and do me a favor? I need you to borrow a can of tomato paste from one of the neighbors."

I put my wish in the drawer and ran down the stairs. "I need paste, not sauce," my mother said.

I ran out the door to Mrs. Kasper's house, saying over and over, "Paste, not sauce." It took Mrs. Kasper a long time to answer the door, so long that I watched a spider catch a fly in a web strung near the porch railing. By the time she finally opened the door, I couldn't remember if my mom wanted tomato paste, not sauce, or sauce, not paste. Mrs. Kasper asked me to step inside while she checked her cupboard.

Something was wrong. Mrs. Kasper did not invite me to sit down. She did not offer me a chocolate-covered cherry. She did not offer me a tiny cup of tea. Her face looked different, too. It looked like mine does when I cry so hard that I hiccup and get a runny nose.

"Were you crying?" I asked Mrs. Kasper.

"Why do you ask, child?"

"Because your face is all blotchy."

"Well, dear, to tell you the truth, I was. You see, today would have been my fifty-third wedding anniversary. I've been sitting here

thinking about my dear departed Walter."

Mrs. Kasper went into the living room and sat down. I wanted to get back home to work on my wish, but she looked so sad I followed her and stood in the doorway. She picked up the gold-framed picture of her and her husband from a table next to the couch.

"He was my life," she said, looking at it.

"Now he's gone and all my friends are dead and even though the years fly by, the days pass so slowly."

"I'm your friend and I'm not dead," I interrupted.

"That's true, you are a special friend," said Mrs. Kasper.

"Mrs. Kasper," I asked, wanting to make her feel better, "would you like to come to my birthday party this afternoon? My mother said I could only have eight people, but Jess can't come, so it would be all right. We're having ice cream cake."

"Thank you, dear, but I can't eat sweets. Doctor's orders."

"We're playing games in the yard," I added.

"The heat bothers me. I prefer to stay indoors," she said.

"You could put your feet in my wading pool to cool off."

Mrs. Kasper laughed. "Oh dear, I think I'd feel naked if I ever took my stockings off in public. Thank you for asking, but I think I'll just stay here and think about Walter."

"He must have been a nice man," I said.

"Oh, he was the finest. He made me feel like a queen. Did you ever wonder why I always have chocolate-covered cherries in my house even though I'm not allowed to eat sweets? I have them because Walter gave me chocolate-covered cherries every birthday. I buy them now just to try to keep Walter here with me."

Mrs. Kasper looked at the picture again. "For forty-seven years this man put laughter in my soul, joy in my heart. He was my reason for living. He's been gone six years now. I've missed out on six years of hugs, six years of kisses, six years of living. Every morning I wake up and wish that this day will be different, that this day I'll start a new life without him, but I can't seem to do it."

She took a hanky from her apron pocket and wiped her eyes. "Enough of this," she said. "Enough." She put the picture on the table and tucked a piece of hair into her hair net.

I sat down next to her. I never realized that old people wish for things, too, just like me. I thought about my crystal and about my birthday party wish. I thought about Mrs. Kasper's wish that she could enjoy living without her dear departed husband.

"Mrs. Kasper," I said, "I have an anniversary present for you." I took the wishing crystal from around my neck and put it over her head. I was careful not to catch it on her hair net. The yarn was a little dirty, but I didn't think she'd mind.

"If it's a magic crystal, it still has a wish

on it. I haven't used it yet," I said. I hugged Mrs. Kasper and went home with a can of tomato paste and a can of sauce.

My party was fun. Everyone loved the favors and the games. The gifts were great, except I didn't get a horse. At the end of the party, as we were all at the picnic table playing a game of Payday that I had gotten from

Amanda, I heard laughing behind me. I looked back and saw my mother and Mrs. Kasper sitting in lawn chairs. Mrs. Kasper was not wearing stockings. She had her feet in the pool.

I smiled. I finally knew for sure that my crystal was a wishing one.

Susan Wojciechowski ★ ★ ★ ★ ★ ★ ★ ★
is the author of *Don't Call Me Beanhead!*,
the first book about Beany, which *School
Library Journal* called "a gem," and the
award-winning *The Christmas Miracle of
Jonathan Toomey*. She was inspired to write
a new story about Beany by her eight-
year-old nephew, Evan, to whom it is ded-
icated. "He is enthralled by the chandelier
in our dining room, so I gave him a crystal
from it and he strung it on a piece of yarn
and wore it around his neck for months
afterward." Susan Wojciechowski lives in
York, Pennsylvania.

Susanna Natti ★ ★ ★ ★ ★ ★ ★ ★ ★
says, "When I was a kid I stuck a joke-
shop suction cup on my head. It was funny
except for the huge red circle it left on my
forehead—and I had to go to school anyway. I remembered that when I read about
Carol Ann fixing up Beany for school pictures. Some adventures can only be laughed
about later." The illustrator of more than
thirty books for children, Susanna Natti lives
in Bedford, Massachusetts.